RIDERS

RESCUE ON TURTLE BEACH

WRITTEN BY JEN MARLIN

ILLUSTRATED BY IZZY BURTON

HARPER

An Imprint of HarperCollinsPublishers

Library of Congress Cataloging-in-Publication Data
Names: Marlin, Jen, author. | Burton, Izzy, 1993- illustrator.
Title: Rescue on turtle beach / Jen Marlin, Izzy Burton.
Description: First edition. | New York, NY : Harper, [2021] | Series: Wind Riders ;
#1 | Audience: Ages 6-10. | Audience: Grades 4-6. | Summary: After discovering
Wind Rider, an abandoned magical sailboat, Max and Sofia arrive on a beach in
Hawaii where, with new friend Laila, they rescue newly hatched sea turtles.
Includes facts about sea turtles.
Identifiers: LCCN 2020052717 | ISBN 978-0-06-302925-5 (hardcover) —
ISBN 978-0-06-302924-8 (paperback)
Subjects: CYAC: Sailboats—Fiction. | Magic—Fiction. | Sea turtles—Fiction. |
Turtles—Fiction. | Wildlife rescue—Fiction. | Hawaii—Fiction.
Classification: LCC PZ7.1.M372445 Res 2021 | DDC [Fic]—dc23
LC record available at https://lccn.loc.gov/2020052717

Typography by Joe Merkel

21 22 23 24 25   PC/LSCC   10 9 8 7 6 5 4 3 2 1

First Edition

For Mark, my hero, who rescues turtles

With special thanks to Erin Falligant

CONTENTS

CHAPTER 1

THE ICE CREAM THIEF

"Ready?" called Grandpa as he picked up the cooler from the back of the truck.

Max gazed at the ocean waves, which sparkled in the afternoon sun. He felt a shiver of excitement. "I'm always ready!" he called, rolling up his hoodie sleeves as he followed Grandpa toward the boats lined up along the dock.

The marina was bustling. It seemed as if everyone in Starry Bay was out and about this sunny afternoon. Kids crowded around the ice cream stand, and families dotted the beach, their bright towels and umbrellas everywhere.

Max spotted a dark-haired girl licking an ice cream cone. He thought of the ice cream sandwiches he and Grandpa had in the cooler, and his mouth watered. The girl was shading her eyes, studying something in the water. But what? Max glanced at the waves but didn't see anything.

As he followed his grandfather onto the dock, he felt the familiar wobble of the boards beneath his feet. The smell of seawater brought a smile to his face.

Grandpa led the way toward his fishing boat, which gleamed in the golden sunlight.

"Hello, old girl," he said. As a retired fisher, Grandpa had spent more of his life on that boat than on dry land. He patted the hull as he stepped aboard.

Max was about to step on board, too, when he heard a yelp. He and Grandpa turned around just in time to see the girl with the ice cream cone dodging a seagull. The bird swooped low, darted toward the cone, and snatched it right out of the girl's hand.

"Hey!" she hollered. "That's mine!"

Grandpa shook his
head. "Pesky seagulls."

When the girl's shoulders
slumped, Max eyed Grandpa's
cooler. "Can I share an ice cream sandwich
with her, Grandpa?" he asked.

Grandpa's eyes crinkled up. "Good
idea," he said. "I need to wipe the boat
down anyway. But don't be too long. When
the tide starts rolling . . ."

"The bass start biting," Max sang back.
"Don't worry, I'll be quick!"

He pulled an ice cream sandwich out of

the cooler and then jogged along the dock. The girl was sitting on a towel now, her chin in her hands. But as Max skidded to a stop beside her, holding out the ice cream, she looked up and smiled.

"Just don't let the birds get this one," Max joked.

The girl laughed. "I love birds, but what a rude seagull! It didn't even say please!"

"Some birds have no manners," said Max. He smoothed down his sandy-brown cowlick and held out his hand. "I'm Max."

The girl grinned as she shook his hand. "I'm Sofia. My parents and I are here for the summer." She nodded toward the ice cream shop, where her parents waved from a wrought-iron table. As she unwrapped

the ice cream sandwich, she noticed Max watching closely.

"Want to split it?" she asked, breaking the sandwich in two.

"Thanks!" He took half of the sandwich, licking the ice cream that had squeezed out from the middle. "I live here with my grandpa. He's getting the boat ready for fishing." When Max gestured toward the dock, Sofia's eyes lit up.

"Do you ever spot sea turtles?" she asked, holding her ice cream sandwich in the air. "I thought I saw one in the water earlier, but it was just seaweed."

Max shook his head. "Sea turtles don't like it much here, now that the beach is so crowded with buildings and people. And they're endangered all over, so there's just less of them than there used to be."

"My mom taught me about that," Sofia said. "She's a veterinarian. She said sea turtles get caught in fishing nets, and sometimes they accidentally eat bits of plastic in the water. It's awful! But I hoped I'd see just one here this summer." She let her gaze drift across the beach, even though she knew there'd be no turtles to spot.

There sure were a lot of seagulls, though.

"Hey!" she said, catching sight of one close by. "Is that the thief that stole my cone?"

As the gull hopped toward them, Max saw a splotch of strawberry ice cream just above the bird's yellow beak. "That's the thief, all right," he said. "It has an ice cream mustache!"

Sofia laughed until she saw the bird was hobbling, leaning toward one side. "Is something wrong with its foot?" she asked with a frown.

Max tiptoed through the sand, following

the seagull. Then he saw a length of string dragging behind it. "Fishing line!" he cried. "It's wrapped around the poor bird's leg." He frowned. Grandpa had taught him never to leave fishing line in the water. Too bad everyone didn't follow that rule.

"We have to help it!" Sofia said, jumping to her feet.

But every time they got close to the gull, it fluttered away. The bird hopped along the beach toward the shady mangrove forest behind the marina. There, it disappeared in a tangle of roots and leaves.

When someone hollered from the beach, Max and Sofia spun around. Sofia's mother waved. "Stay close!" she called, cupping her mouth with a hand.

"We will!" shouted Sofia.

Max checked over his shoulder for Grandpa. He was hunched over the deck of the boat, untangling a rope, which meant Max had a few more minutes to spare before they set sail.

When he turned back to Sofia, she was already gone, sprinting after the injured gull.

"Wait for me!" Max cried, racing after

her. He hopped down onto a dirt path and into the shade, where the air was moist and cool. He slowed to a jog, careful not to trip over the thick roots of the mangrove trees.

When Max reached Sofia, she was standing perfectly still, staring between two thick clumps of palms. "Do you see the gull?" he asked, leaning over to catch his breath.

Sofia shook her head.

"But look," she whispered.

Max peered through the thick fronds and hanging moss. A sailboat rested at an odd angle, half in the water and half beached on the sand. Its tattered sail flapped in the breeze, as if calling them forward.

Max had told Grandpa he'd be back soon, but he couldn't resist. "Come on," he whispered.

CHAPTER 2
WIND RIDER

Max examined the neglected boat. Navy-blue paint was chipping off the wooden boards of the hull. The torn, yellowing sail hung over the deck rail, covering the faded white letters that were painted on the bow. Max lifted the sail and Sofia came closer to read them.

"*Wind Rider*," she murmured.

"You can tell it used to be a nice boat," Max said thoughtfully, tracing the sun-bleached *W* with his finger. "Why would anyone abandon it?"

Sofia didn't answer. She was too busy finding the quickest way on board.

Max turned just in time to see her climbing a creaky metal ladder hanging on the side of the boat onto the deck.

"Sofia, wait!" he called. "It might not be safe!" He pictured the rotting boards of the deck and the creatures that might have made themselves at home below, like alligators, snakes, or even bears!

But Sofia was already tugging on the rusty metal handle to a wooden hatch leading below deck. There was a *snap*. "Oops," she said, staring at the handle in her hand.

Max climbed over the deck rail. Something dove toward him, ruffling his brown hair. The seagull landed a few feet away from Sofia and bobbed its head.

Then it flapped its wings just enough to fly to the helm, the wooden steering wheel near the stern of the boat. As the bird shifted its weight, the wheel creaked left and then right.

"Hey!" Max stared in wonder. "It's the seagull!" He pointed toward the fishing line still wrapped around the gull's leg.

Sofia's heart leaped at the sight. "Maybe it knows we want to help it."

The bird watched her carefully as she stepped toward the helm.

Sofia paused.

"My mom and I saved a bird with an injured wing once," she said. She remembered how her mother had gently wrapped the bird in a towel to calm it down. "Do we have a towel or something?"

Max scanned the deck of the ship. Not spotting anything useful, he pulled off his hoodie. "Use this," he said.

"Perfect."

Sofia took it and crept toward the seagull. When the bird was within reach, she gently tossed the hoodie over its head. "It's okay," she crooned, quickly gathering it into her arms. The bird felt surprisingly light. It squawked only once before quieting down.

"Wow," said Max. "You're really good with animals."

Sofia felt a flush of pride.

"Can you hold it?" she asked. She passed the bundled bird to Max, who cradled it carefully.

Max watched as Sofia carefully unwound the fishing line from the bird's leg. When she was done, he set the bird back on the helm and removed the hoodie.

The gull gazed at him and Sofia for another moment, then seemed to nod at them with an approving "Caw!"

Suddenly, it flapped its wide wings and took off. Max jumped backward, losing his balance. He grasped at the spokes of the helm to steady himself, but it was too late. He tumbled to the deck.

"Are you okay?" Sofia asked, leaning down to help him up.

Max stared at the helm.

The moment he'd grabbed the wheel, it had begun to spin. But instead of slowing down now after he let go, it seemed to be speeding up. It went faster and faster, until the spokes blurred together.

Sofia's mouth dropped open. "It's spinning by itself," she whispered.

Just then, a gust of wind nearly knocked her off her feet. "Whoa!" she said. "What's happening?"

Max felt it, too. Was a storm brewing? Wind howled through the mangrove forest. Then the torn-up sail flapped against Max's face. He pushed it away and grabbed the deck rail.

"Hang on . . . ," he started to say, squinting at the wind, which swallowed up his words.

Sofia gripped the rail with both hands and dropped low. She squeezed her eyes shut, waiting for the storm to pass.

Then, just as suddenly as it had begun, the howling stopped. The boat rocked gently from side to side.

Sofia opened one eye. She pushed her dark bangs out of her face, pulled herself upright, and opened the other one. As she gazed over the rail, she sucked in her breath. Instead of sand and mangrove trees, she saw . . . *water.* "Look!" she cried.

Max rose, too, on wobbly legs. He spun

in a slow circle, searching for the mangrove forest. For the beach or the marina. For any land at all.

But there were only clear skies and bright blue waves all the way to the horizon.

"We're sailing," Sofia whispered, a smile slowly spreading across her face.

Max's heart raced, as fast as the sailboat beneath his feet. Because it was true. Somehow, he and Sofia had left Starry Bay.

And now they were sailing, all alone, across a calm, open sea.

CHAPTER 3

LAND HO!

"Do you see land *anywhere*?" Max asked, shading his eyes.

Sofia shook her head. The waves glittered like crystals under the dazzling afternoon sun. The deck rocked gently beneath her feet, and she glanced down. "Hey, look!"

Max leaned over the rail, following her gaze to where *Wind Rider* was painted across the side of the boat. Each bright white letter stood out clearly against the navy-blue hull.

"The paint looks brand-new!" he cried.

"*Everything* looks brand-new," said Sofia, staring at the crisp white sail billowing overhead.

"But how?" asked Max.

"I have no idea," said Sofia. "But I want to see more!" She turned toward the hatch that led belowdecks. The metal

handle that she'd broken off was fixed and shone brightly against the smooth wooden planks. She grabbed it and threw open the hatch.

She scurried down the ladder into the cabin, shaking her head in wonder, with Max right behind.

Golden afternoon sunlight poured through the portholes, casting a warm glow inside. Pots and pans gleamed, hanging from hooks above a sink. Four chairs were pushed neatly against a long wooden table. And books stood straight and tall on a shelf, their spines like a colorful picket fence.

Sofia ran her finger along them, reading the titles: *The Ultimate Nature Guide. By Land or By Sea. Amazing Animals A to Z.* Something clomped across the room, making Sofia jump.

"You scared me!" she said, giggling.

"Where'd you get that?"

Max laughed from behind the snorkeling mask. He took a clumsy step, tripping over the blue fins on his feet.

"Chell it ow!" he said.

"Huh?" Sofia raised her eyebrows.

He pulled the snorkeling mask down. "Sorry. Check it out!" he said again. "That sea chest is full of diving and snorkeling stuff."

Sofia looked behind him. A large wooden chest sat snugly between an armchair and some stately wooden shelves. It reminded her of the kind of treasure chest you might read about in a book, but this one had been carved with delicate etchings of dolphins, crabs, birds, and all other kinds of animals. Just then, something caught Max's eye through one of the portholes. He stepped closer, peering through the glass. Rocky cliffs rose up in the distance. "Land ho!" he cried.

Sofia nudged him aside so that she could see, too. "Where are we?" she asked, studying the sandy cove at the base of the cliffs.

Smack! An atlas lying on the table beside her suddenly flipped open. Its pages turned

as if they'd been caught in a strong wind. When they settled, Sofia stared at the map spread out in the book before her. It showed a string of green islands in a blue sea.

"Hawaii?" she asked, looking at the map in

astonishment. "Did we just sail to Hawaii?"

"Why not?" Max asked. After all, if an old sailboat could become new and somehow sail itself, why couldn't it take them to a Hawaiian island?

Sofia laughed out loud as she hurried up the ladder to the deck. She raced toward the bow as the boat glided into the cove.

Max joined her, his snorkeling mask dangling around his neck. In his hands, he carried his fins and the other gear he'd picked up from the sea chest.

Sofia pointed at a tall, narrow, bright

white building with a round red top perched on the edge of the cliff. "There's a lighthouse up there!" she said.

"And there's something on the beach," said Max, studying a large building that rose up above a grove of palm trees. He squinted to read the banner above the doorway: "'The Aloha Inn—Grand Opening.'"

"*Aloha* Inn?" Sofia repeated. "We're definitely in Hawaii!"

Wind Rider gave a sudden lurch, and Sofia and Max braced themselves against the rail.

"What happened?" Sofia asked.

"The boat dropped its anchor," said Max. "I guess this is as far as it's going to take us."

"So . . . now what?" asked Sofia. She put her foot on the rail. The water below looked calm, and it rippled with deep blues and bright greens.

A few feet away from the boat, Max saw something pop up from the water. It disappeared almost right away, but he knew what he had seen. He glanced at Sofia and grinned. She hadn't spotted it yet.

"I think there's something down there you should look at," he said mysteriously.

Then he handed her a snorkeling mask and fins.

Sofia hesitated. She had never snorkeled before, but . . . how hard could it be?

As she tugged on the fins, she heard a splash. Max's head appeared in the water below. He put on his mask and waved at Sofia to follow. As he put his face back into the water and began to swim, his orange snorkel bobbed along the water's surface.

He found himself in a world lit with brilliant color. Clusters of pink, yellow, and fire-red plants grew along every surface.

A coral reef! He glanced around, trying to spot what he'd seen before.

Up above, Sofia put her own snorkel in her mouth, straightened her mask, and jumped into the water. *Let's do this!* she thought, giving a swift kick with her fins.

As she dipped herself into the water, she saw a school of tropical fish dart past, so close that she could have reached out and touched their orange stripes. She followed Max toward the colorful reef.

That was when she saw him waving frantically at her and pointing just to her left. She could suddenly sense something large swimming beside her.

Sofia held her breath and turned slowly.

When she saw the smooth shell and black-spotted head, her heart leaped in her chest.

A sea turtle!

The creature was almost as long as Sofia, with big front flippers that cut through the water like the oars of a rowing boat. Golds, greens, and warm browns shimmered across its shell, and its big eyes shone with curiosity as its gaze passed over her.

It moved as if in slow motion.

As soon as Sofia surfaced, she whipped the snorkel out of her mouth. She looked for Max. "That was so cool!" she cried. "I didn't just *see* a sea turtle. I *swam* with one!"

Max grinned. "I know," he said. "It was so—"

A shout suddenly rang out across the open water.

Sofia spun around. "What was that?"

Max pointed to a girl on the beach, who was crouched in the sand.

"Is she okay?" asked Sofia.

"I don't know," said Max, worried. "But *something's* going on."

There was only one way to find out what. They both kicked for shore.

CHAPTER 4

THE TiNY TURTLE

Carrying their fins and masks, Max and Sofia raced along the beach toward the girl.

"Is everything all right?" Sofia asked as they approached her. Sofia leaned over to catch her breath.

The girl shook her head, her thick black

braid swaying from shoulder to shoulder. "A baby sea turtle hatched from its nest." She pointed toward a low mesh fence in the sand. Sofia had seen fences like this before. They were noticeable enough to keep people off the nest but flexible enough for the animals that lived there to get in and out.

"It's running the wrong way!" the girl said. "I'm trying to lead it to the water before it gets lost."

"A baby sea turtle?" Sofia gasped. "Where?" She tiptoed forward, searching the sand.

"Here!" said Max. He crouched low to get a better look at the baby turtle, which was only about the length of a stick of bubble gum. Its whole body wobbled back and forth as it scrambled across the sand on its flippers. But the girl was right—it was running for the trees instead of the water!

Thinking quickly, Max gently blocked the turtle's path with a piece

of driftwood. Sofia used her foot to scoop a path through the sand. The path sloped downward, straight to the water's edge. "C'mon, little buddy," she said in a soothing voice. "This way."

The girl with the braid squatted by the path to help keep the turtle on track. As Max watched in wonder, the turtle began to scurry down the beach, faster and faster,

toward the water. "It's working," he said under his breath. "We did it!"

When a wave rolled in, the water scooped up the baby turtle, and soon it was swimming safely out to sea. "Yes!" cried Max.

"Yay!" yelled Sofia. She turned to give the girl with the braid a high five.

"Thank you," said the girl. "You showed up just in time!" She gave a shy smile. "I'm Laila. My mom and I live just down the beach. Are you staying here at the hotel?"

Sofia glanced up at the Aloha Inn. "Um, no, we're not. I'm Sofia, and this is Max." She pointed toward Max, and then realized he was gone. "Max?"

"Over here!" He stood beside the mesh fence, staring down at the turtle nest. It looked like a mound of sand. "Why did only one turtle hatch?" he asked. "There should be dozens of eggs in there. But there's only one set of footprints—er, I mean *flipper* prints!"

Sofia ran to join him. "Maybe it hatched

early. My mom told me most sea turtles hatch at night."

Max nodded. "I hope the other turtles don't hatch until after the sun sets. They look for the moonlight on the water, and that's how they find their way."

Laila cleared her throat. "I don't think hatching tonight would be a good idea at all . . . ," she said.

Sofia whirled around. "What do you mean?"

Laila twisted her braid around her finger and then pointed at the Aloha Inn.

"The inn is having a grand opening party tonight. In a few hours, it will be all lit up!"

Max sucked in his breath.

"What?" asked Sofia. "What's wrong?"

"The baby turtles might get confused by the hotel lights," said Max. "They'll head *away* from the water instead of toward it!" He began to pace the length of the mesh fence. "It's called light pollution," he said. "It's one reason why sea turtles are endangered. And why there were so few turtles to see back home in Starry Bay."

"So what do we do?" Sofia asked.

No one answered. Silence fell over the beach. Beneath the late afternoon sun, waves lapped gently against the shore.

Max kicked at the sand with his toe. "I wish there was a way to make the ocean brighter."

Laila spun around slowly. "I think I have an idea," she said.

As she stared up at the rocky cliffs surrounding the cove, a slow smile spread across her face.

CHAPTER 5
THE LigHTHOUSE

Sofia followed Laila's gaze toward the cliffs. She squinted, and then she saw it—the tall white tower with the round red top. "The lighthouse!" she shouted.

"Phew!" breathed Max. "With the lighthouse there, there's no problem. When the light reflects on the water, it'll be brighter than the hotel. Bright enough to guide the baby turtles."

Laila's face fell. "But there *is* a problem," she said. "I've never seen the light turned on."

Max and Sofia frowned.

"I've heard that the old lighthouse keeper still lives there," Laila continued, "but I've never met him."

"He'll turn the light on for us," Sofia said, with as much confidence as she could drum up. "I mean, for the baby turtles. Won't he?"

Laila bit her lip. "Maybe, but . . . we would need a boat to reach that part of the cove."

Max smiled. "We've got that covered," he said. "C'mon!"

A few minutes later, with the help of the Aloha Inn's dinghy, they were climbing up *Wind Rider*'s metal ladder. Max expertly secured the dinghy to *Wind Rider* with some rope.

"Is this *your* boat?" Laila asked as soon as they were all on deck. "Where are your parents? Who sails it?"

Before Max could answer, a chain rattled from the bow of the boat. The anchor came up, and the sail lines tightened. With a snap, the sail caught wind, and the helm of the boat began to spin.

Laila gasped. "It's magic!"

Sofia and Max shared a smile.

"It is," said Sofia, the secret spilling from

her lips. "We found it beached near a man-grove forest back home. It brought us here. We don't really know how or why."

"Well, I know why," Laila announced. "The boat brought you here to save the turtles!"

Max locked eyes with Sofia.

She nodded as she realized that Laila could be right. After all, they *had* arrived just in time to help their new friend guide the first baby turtle to safety.

But as long shadows from the cliffs fell across the deck, Sofia shivered. "It'll be dark out in a few hours. If we're going to save the turtles, we'd better act fast." *Wind Rider* sped through the waves as if it heard her words.

As soon as *Wind Rider* got close to the lighthouse, Laila jumped onto a rickety dock and tied the boat to a thick metal cleat. Max and Sofia followed her, and the three of them hurried toward the rocky path that led to the lighthouse.

Max gazed upward. "It's really steep," he said.

Laila turned, waiting for Max and Sofia

to catch up. "We have some of the tallest sea cliffs in the world here in Hawaii," she said. "They were made by volcanoes millions of years ago."

Millions of years? thought Max, squinting up at the tops of the cliffs in awe. He reached out to touch the old rock.

"Look out!" Sofia cried, pointing to a tiny creature the size of a golf ball, hiding in the crevice of a rock. Its hard, spiky body was dark purple and covered in pointy spines.

"A sea urchin!" Max drew his hand back. "Grandpa says a sea urchin's feet are like suction cups that help it hold on."

As his own foot slipped on the wet rocks below, he gave a nervous laugh. "I wish I had suction-cup feet right now, too."

"Be careful," Laila said. "They really hurt if you get pricked by one."

Max nodded.

They continued to scamper over the rocks, slowing down only to avoid stepping on the wildflowers growing in between the moss-covered rocks.

At the top of the cliff, the lighthouse towered above them. The waves crashed against the shore below. Laila led the way toward the small house that stood beside the tower. When they reached the front step, she nodded nervously at Max and Sofia, then knocked on the door.

Max held his breath as the door creaked open. Light spilled across the doorstep, and an old man with weathered skin and a head of bushy white hair stood before them.

"Yes?" he said. His voice cracked.

"We're here to talk to you about the lighthouse," said Laila, stepping forward.

"We need you to turn the light on!" Max jumped in.

"Please help us!" Sofia added dramatically.

The old man's eyes narrowed. "That light is of no use to anyone anymore," he said. "And neither am I. Now go away."

He shut the door so quickly, Max jumped backward, bumping into Sofia.

Sofia felt the hope that had carried them all the way up that steep, rocky cliff suddenly disappear, like the sun that was dipping below the horizon. Any moment now, the baby turtles might hatch. And there'd be no one there to save them.

CHAPTER 6
NOT ON MY WATCH

"I can't believe the lighthouse keeper won't help us!" Laila whispered, breaking the silence.

"I hope we didn't freak him out," Sofia said thoughtfully.

"I know he was really rude, but I feel kind

of sorry for him," said Max. "He's right that lighthouses aren't needed much anymore. They used to save a lot of lives. But now, boats like Grandpa's have electronic equipment to help guide them to shore."

Sofia lifted her chin, determined not to be defeated. "We have to try and talk to him again." She took a deep breath and banged on the door. "Please, sir, we need to talk to you. Your lighthouse can save lives again—*tonight*—if you'll just help us!" She waited, crossing her fingers.

The door cracked open again and Sofia's heart leaped.

"What lives?" the old man asked, studying her face.

"Baby turtles!" Laila blurted. "Near the Aloha Inn. They're hatching, but the inn's having a big party and the lights will confuse them. They'll get lost. But your lighthouse can save them. Its beacon can guide them out to sea!"

The lighthouse keeper's forehead creased with worry. "Sea turtles are beautiful animals," he said. "They've been here a very long time. They're much older than humans. They're even older than dinosaurs."

"And now they're in danger of going extinct," Max said.

The lighthouse keeper shook his head. "Not on my watch," he said firmly. He flung the door open wide and stepped out. "C'mon, follow me."

As the old man led them to the lighthouse, Max pumped his fist in the air.

At the lighthouse, the man fiddled with a set of keys. With a *click* and a *creak*, the heavy door swung open. He grabbed a flashlight that hung on the wall and flicked it on, lighting up the room. They were at the bottom of a spiraling flight of wooden stairs.

White paint peeled from the brick walls of the lighthouse. The air was thick with the smell of must and salt water. The spiral staircase ahead beckoned.

"Careful!" called the old man as Sofia raced toward the stairs.

Sofia tried to slow down, but her feet wouldn't listen. The turtles needed her! Step after step, around and around, she sprinted up the stairs. Finally, she could see the stone landing at the top.

Then, *crack!* The world fell out from under Sofia's feet. She cried out, lunging for the wooden stair rail.

Max looked up in time to see a foot dangling through the rotted wooden step above. "Sofia!" he shouted.

"I'm okay," Sofia called back down. A moment later, the foot disappeared as she scrambled up onto the next stair. *Phew*, she thought. *That was a close one.*

When the others reached her, Max's stomach sank. Sofia stood above a set of broken stairs, and he and the others stood below.

"Can you all climb over them?" Sofia asked.

The lighthouse keeper shook his head,

frowning. "No," he said. "We shouldn't go any farther. I shouldn't have brought you this far. You could have been badly hurt. Can you get back down?"

Sofia nodded. "I can, but . . . what about the turtles?"

The lighthouse keeper was about to argue. But Sofia looked deadly serious. "I can do it," she said with determination.

The lighthouse keeper took a deep breath. "All right. Go through the door. The beacon's just inside that room. There's a big red switch on the wall that turns it on. Flip it up. But be careful!"

Sofia wasted no time. She held her breath and gripped the wooden rail as she took the last few steps toward the landing.

Max paused by a tiny window on the staircase. The sun had nearly set. In the distance, lights began to flicker into life. "The hotel is turning on its lights!" he cried. "Hurry, Sofia!"

"I'm trying!" she called back. She was in the round room that held the beacon, trying to flip the red switch. But it had rusted in the salty sea air. It wouldn't budge.

You can do this, Sofia told herself.

With a grunt, she heaved the switch upward. Finally, it gave way beneath her fingers. But the room was still cloaked in darkness.

Sofia's heart sank.

Had she broken the switch? If she had, there'd be no way to save the turtles. And the babies would be hatching any minute!

CHAPTER 7
RACE TO THE BEACH

Below, Max, Laila, and the lighthouse keeper nervously waited.

"What's going on?" he called up to Sofia. "Did it work?"

Suddenly, bright, blinding light poured through the staircase window. "You did it!" he cried. "Sofia, you did it!"

"It's so bright," said Laila, shielding her eyes. "The baby turtles will see it for sure!"

Sofia's flushed face appeared on the landing above. "Let's go!" she said. "We have to get back to the beach!"

"Steady," the lighthouse keeper reminded her as he reached for her hand.

"Let's get you there in one piece. And let's try to keep the stairway in one piece, too!"

He helped her step over the rotted boards. Then they hurried back down toward the door.

At the bottom, the lighthouse keeper paused.

"Good luck, kids," he said with a nod. "I really hope this works."

"Thanks!" said Max. He started to race out the door, but then he stopped. "And thanks for helping us."

"I'll come back to tell you how it all turns out," Laila promised the old man.

The man's eyes crinkled into a smile. "If it works, I'll make sure the light is on *every* night through turtle-hatching season."

"Thank you!" said Sofia, grinning.

With one last round of goodbyes, they left the lighthouse keeper in the doorway. Max thought the man was standing a little taller as the light from his lighthouse led them safely back down the rocky trail to their boat.

• • •

As *Wind Rider* crossed the waves toward the turtle nest, bright lights and party music poured from the doors of the Aloha Inn. "Will the lighthouse be bright enough?" Laila asked as she glanced over her shoulder.

"It *has* to be!" said Sofia.

With a jolt, *Wind Rider* dropped anchor. Max hoped they wouldn't have to swim too far to get to shore. But this time, the boat had anchored beside a long pier that led to the sandy beach. "C'mon!" he called to the others.

Together, they stepped down onto the pier and raced toward the mesh fence surrounding the turtle nest. Sofia got there first, just as a tiny gray head popped out of the sand. "It's happening!" she whispered.

The baby turtle squirmed side to side,

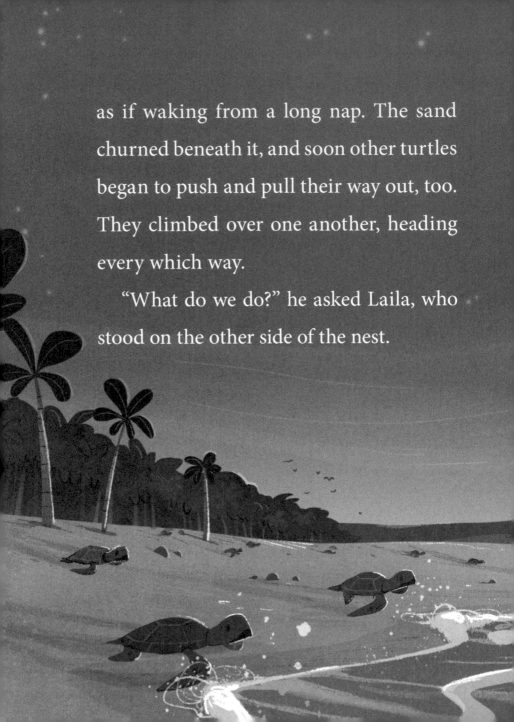

as if waking from a long nap. The sand churned beneath it, and soon other turtles began to push and pull their way out, too. They climbed over one another, heading every which way.

"What do we do?" he asked Laila, who stood on the other side of the nest.

Laila chewed her lip. "Just wait," she whispered.

Sofia waited, holding her breath. Soon, the beach was covered with baby turtles— and they were stumbling away from the hotel's party lights!

"It's working!" whispered Max.

Slowly but surely, the turtles had begun to scurry toward the brilliant beam of the lighthouse, reflecting off the water like the biggest, brightest full moon ever!

"They're doing it!" Sofia whispered.

The turtles rolled toward the water's edge, where the waves scooped them up and carried them safely out to sea.

Sofia laughed with relief. "They made it. They all made it!"

"Wait!" Laila called from back at the nest. "There's one more. Its eggshell is stuck!"

Sofia hurried over to where a tiny turtle

was struggling through the sand. Its round, white eggshell was dragging from its back flipper.

Gently, Laila reached down and grabbed ahold of the eggshell. With one last tug, the turtle broke free. It scampered quickly after the others, like it was saying, *Guys! Guys! Wait for me!*

Max cheered.

Caw! Caw!

"No!" Laila gasped, looking up at the sky. "A seagull is after the turtle!"

Sofia lurched forward, trying to shield

the baby turtle with her body.

"Sofia, it's okay!" Max called to her. "That's not just any seagull. It's *our* seagull."

Laila's eyes widened. "*Your* seagull?"

"It led us to *Wind Rider* back home," Max explained. "Somehow it knew we needed to come here, to help you save the turtles."

Sofia glanced up. "Are you sure that's it?" she asked. She watched as the gull swooped low and landed at Max's feet.

When it bobbed its head in greeting, just like it had when they first met, Max laughed out loud. "I'm sure."

"But why is it here now?" asked Laila.

Max frowned. "Maybe it's because we did what it brought us here to do," he said. "We saved the turtles. Now I think it's telling us it's time to go home."

Laila sighed. "I should get home, too. My mom will be worried."

Sofia waited until the last baby turtle disappeared into the water. Then she stood up, looking sad. "I don't want to say goodbye," she said.

Laila threw her arms around Sofia and

gave her a great big hug. "The turtles will be back," she said. "They'll return to this same beach to lay their own eggs someday."

Sofia grinned. "That's right!" she said. "And maybe we'll come back someday, too." The turtles would live for a hundred years. That meant Max and Sofia had a whole lot of time to get back to Hawaii and see the turtles they saved lay their own eggs!

"I hope you'll come back," said Laila. Then she held something out to her new friends.

Sofia gasped. It was the eggshell that

Laila had pulled from the baby turtle's flipper! The shell was the size and shape of a Ping-Pong ball, and it was nearly cracked in half.

Laila carefully separated the eggshell into two pieces. She tucked one half in Sofia's palm and held on to the other. "To help you remember today," she said.

"Like we could ever forget," said Sofia. She gently rubbed the shell. It wasn't hard like a chicken's egg, but soft, like leather.

Sofia passed the bit of shell to Max, and he held it up to admire it. As it caught the light from the lighthouse, the shell glowed white and round in the night sky. "It looks like a full moon!" said Max.

"Maybe it'll lead you home," said Laila. She gave them each a quick hug. Then she hurried down the pier, waving goodbye.

Sofia promised herself that when she came back to visit the turtles, she would see Laila again, too . . . however old they all were.

CHAPTER 8
ANOTHER ADVENTURE

Back on *Wind Rider,* Sofia went below to find a safe place to put the broken turtle egg Laila had given them. She chose one of the wooden shelves next to the carved sea chest. The eggshell would be safe there, and she knew that every time she and Max saw it, they'd be reminded of this magical trip to Hawaii.

When Sofia climbed back up the steps, she saw that *Wind Rider* was sliding slowly out of the cove and back into open water. She joined Max by the deck rail. The beam from the lighthouse flickered on the waves ahead, but no land was in sight.

"Are you sure we can get back home like this?" she asked Max.

He stepped up to the rail beside her. "The boat knows what to do. I can feel it," he said.

Moments later, a familiar gust of wind sent Sofia's hair blowing across her face. When the deck beneath her feet lurched, she smiled widely. "Here we go," she said.

Max had already gripped the rail. As the helm began to spin, he crouched low and called out, "Time to ride the wind!"

As the deck rocked and the wind howled, Max squeezed his eyes shut and imagined the marina at Starry Bay. It had been an amazing adventure, but he was ready to go home.

Then, just as suddenly as it had

whipped up, the wind died down, and the boat was still.

Max opened his eyes to daylight drenching the deck. But the boat's smooth planks looked weathered and warped again, and the tattered sail hung at a tilt. They were back where they'd started, in the mangrove forest.

Sofia shielded her eyes and looked up at the sky. "The sun hasn't moved," she said. "It's like no time has passed at all."

Max's freckled face broke into a smile. "Maybe it hasn't," he said. "Anything is possible when you've got a magic boat."

As they climbed off *Wind Rider*'s deck onto solid ground, Max turned to give the hull one last pat. "I hope we can go on another adventure soon," he said.

"Yes!" cried Sofia. "And maybe we can help other animals in trouble. But . . . how will we know when they need us?"

Caw, caw!

The seagull flew over her shoulder, so close that she felt the flap of its wings. As Sofia ducked, she laughed out loud.

Max grinned. "I'm pretty sure our feathered friend will let us know when it's time to come back to the boat."

With one last *caw*, the gull flew over
the mangrove forest toward the marina.
Max and Sofia followed, pushing their way
through the tangle of trees. When they
came out into the open, everything seemed
to be exactly the way they'd left it.

"Mom and Dad are still there!" she said in disbelief. "We've been gone for hours, but they're still at the ice cream stand."

"So it's true," Max said. "We really did come back to the moment we left. That must be part of the magic. And it means Grandpa must still be on the boat!" He glanced over at the dock. Sure enough, Grandpa had just untied his fishing boat, the long rope wound around his hand. With his other hand, he waved his cap— his sign to Max that it was time to do some fishing.

"I've gotta go," said Max. He started toward the dock, but then he turned around. "Hey, do you want to go for another ride?" he asked Sofia. "Grandpa's fishing boat isn't magic, but it's still pretty cool."

Sofia grinned. "Definitely!"

She raced toward the marina to ask her parents, with Max close behind. And soon after they were scrambling down the dock toward the water, like baby turtles heading out to sea.

THE WIND RIDER LOGBOOK

Sofia's sketch of *Wind Rider*

caBin

hELm

STeRh

hull

mast

SeaGull

Sail

porThole

bow

WindRIDER

anchor

OUR HAWAii ADVENTURE

Kauai

Oahu

Wind Rider brought us to Hawaii, which
is made up of 137 islands in the Pacific
Ocean. It has a warm, tropical climate and
active volcanoes. All kinds of animals live
on the islands and in the waters, including
sea turtles, sharks, manta rays, and bats.
But sadly, it has more endangered species
than any other state in the USA. Plastic

pollution is a big problem, with lots of
waste products dumped into the sea.
It's dangerous for wildlife and bad for
the environment.

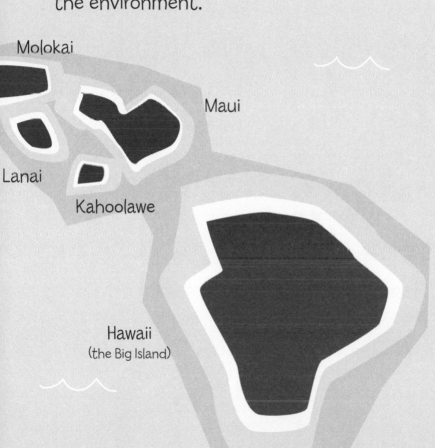

Molokai

Maui

Lanai

Kahoolawe

Hawaii
(the Big Island)

MAX'S SEA TURTLE FACTS

We met some beautiful sea turtles in Hawaii.
Here are my top sea turtle facts!

■ Sea turtles lay their
eggs on the beaches
by tropical seas.
But they travel long
distances to feed,
sometimes crossing
whole oceans.

■ The biggest leatherback sea turtles can each weigh as much as a grand piano!

■ Six out of the seven types of sea turtle are endangered.

■ Turtles can get accidentally caught in fishing nets, and their nests are sometimes disturbed by beach construction.

■ In some places, they're even hunted for their meat.

HOW CAN WE HELP SAVE THE SEA TURTLES?

If you live near the coast, you could join a coastal cleanup project and remove garbage from the beach to protect sea turtles' nesting sites.

When near a nesting site, turn off any lights after dark to help baby turtles find their way to the sea.

If you eat fish, make sure it has been caught in a responsible way that doesn't harm sea turtles.

Use less plastic! Lots of plastic waste, which is harmful to many animals, ends up in the sea. Plastic straws can end up stuck in the nostrils of sea turtles—so avoid straws, or use ones made from biodegradable materials.